A Prom

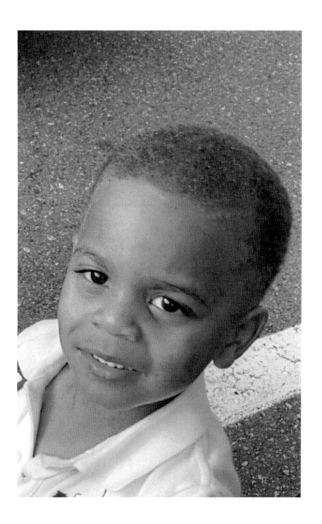

Introduction

In a child's world, a promise is a very important thing. Eli expresses how important it is by praying about a promise which was made to him by an important person. People can be faulty and break commitments to others, sometimes without even realizing what it does to the one who received the promise. But, Jesus never breaks his promises, He keeps them forever and children can trust that.

Every week, the Sabbath day is a special occasion for Eli and his family. On the Sabbath day, his grandma and grandpa would bring a special dish for the family to enjoy.

A delicious Sabbath Supper

Oh....., how Eli loved to spend time with his grandparents because they told him many true stories which greatly excited Eli.

Eli and his family frequently took nature walks, they lived on a large country property with many trees, farm animals and blooming flowers.

On this particular Sabbath afternoon, Eli asked his Grandmother, "can we walk a different path next Sabbath, I'd like to see the pond in the back?" Grandma said, "I promise, we will go!".

All week Eli talked about the next Sabbath. He looked forward to the nature walk and dinner he would have with his grandparents.

When Sabbath arrived, Eli noticed that his grandparents had not arrived at the usual time.

At least an hour had passed and grandpa and grandma still had not arrived. Eli grew sad and wondered what happened.

He could not understand why grandma didn't keep her promise to be there at 9 o'clock. Eli tried to remember a time when Grandma had ever broke her promise to him, but he could not!

The clock was ticking and time was passing and Eli was eagerly awaiting, so he decided to ask Jesus what happened to Grandma?

Eli went to his room, closed the door, and walked over to his small bible, opened it and prayed, (Dear Jesus, you always keep your promises, can you help grandma to be like you and keep her promise?)

HOLY BIBLE

Eli got up and opened his Bible to the verse they had read last night. In it he found Hebrews 6:15, which says,

"And so, after he had patiently endured, he obtained the pro....

(there was a knock at the door)."

Boom Boom!!

And before Eli finished reading the word promise, he heard a knock at the door again.

Eli jumped up and ran to the door, and opened it, amazingly stood Grandma.

Eli was filled with so much joy. He said, "Grandma I thought you were going to break your promise" she said, "men may fail us, but Jesus never does!"

The End

For more information or
copies, please email us at
amlaelle@charter.net

Made in the USA
Columbia, SC
10 November 2022

70257630R00015